USBORNE ENGLIS

PUNCTUATION PUZZLES

Robyn Gee and Peter McClelland
Edited by Jenny Tyler
Designed and illustrated by Graham Round

Introducing punctuation

Punctuation is a collection of marks used in writing to make it easier for whoever reads it to understand it.

When you speak, there are all sorts of things you do to help to make the meaning of your words clear to other people. You can make your voice go higher or lower, louder or softer, faster or slower; you can leave short or long gaps, or pauses, between groups of words; you can change the expression on your face. When you write, punctuation has to do all this for you.

Get in the habit of reading through anything you have written to see whether you can make it clearer by using punctuation. The puzzles in this book will help you to practise using it. Below are the punctuation marks you will meet and when to use them.

Full stop

A full stop tells you where to leave a gap, or pause, when you are reading. You use it at the end of a sentence. A sentence is a word, or a group of words, that makes complete sense on its own.

Question mark

A question mark is used instead of a full stop at the end of a sentence that asks a question.

Comma

A comma tells you when to leave a short pause when you are reading. It marks a much shorter pause than a full stop.

Exclamation mark

An exclamation mark is used at the end of a sentence to mark surprise or excitement.

Apostrophe

An apostrophe looks like a comma, but you put it near the top of letters, instead of on the line you are writing on. It can show that something belongs to someone, or that a word has been shortened and had letters missed out.

Inverted commas

You use inverted commas when you write the exact words that someone has spoken.

Capital letters

Every letter can be written as a capital letter, or a small letter. Most of the time you should use small letters in your writing, but there are certain places where you should use capitals. At the start of a sentence you should always use a capital letter.

Spaces

It is important to leave a good space between each word, otherwise people will find your writing hard to read.

There are hints on each page to remind you of these rules.

When you finish a puzzle check your answers on pages 28 to 32.

Grandpa Og's birthday party

In this book you will meet a family called the Ogs and their friends. They live in Reptile Road, Ogtown. Here they are celebrating Grandpa Og's birthday. There are a number of full stops, question marks, exclamation marks, commas and inverted commas hidden in the picure. See how many of each punctuation mark you can find. Write the answers at the bottom of the page.

_____ Full stops _____ Question marks _____ Commas

_____ Exclamation marks _____ Pairs of Inverted commas

Meet the Og family

Grandma Og

Grandma Og is a potter. She makes bowls and mugs and plates for her family to use. When she writes, she uses too many full stops.

Grandpa Og

Grandpa Og enjoys birdwatching. Every day he puts some scraps out for the birds. When he writes, he uses too many capital letters.

Mrs. Og

Mrs. Og does wonderful paintings of animals. Sometimes she decorates caves with them. She forgets to use full stops.

Mr. Og

Mr. Og grows his own vegetables and collects berries and plants to cook with. He always forgets to use question marks when he writes.

Mog Og

Mog loves writing. She keeps a diary and has started her own newspaper with the help of her family. When she writes, she forgets to use capital letters.

Zog Og

Zog Og is learning to play the drums. He is a fan of the Ogtown Bashers' bodyball team. He does not leave spaces between words when he writes.

The Og family are helping to organize the annual Ogtown firework party. They have all made notices to let the people of Ogtown know about this event. Can you work out which one of the family wrote each notice? Write the notices out correctly on their empty posters.

You will see rockets and sparklers, catherine wheels and roman candles, and lots, lots more.

There will be a firework party. on Saturday ight. at the illtop Arena.

Bring Some fOod anD drInk and wear Your warmEst clotheS.

the party starts at sunset. don't be late!

Are you bored Do you want some fun Why not come to our firework party

There will be a brass band Entry is free Bring some wood for the bonfire

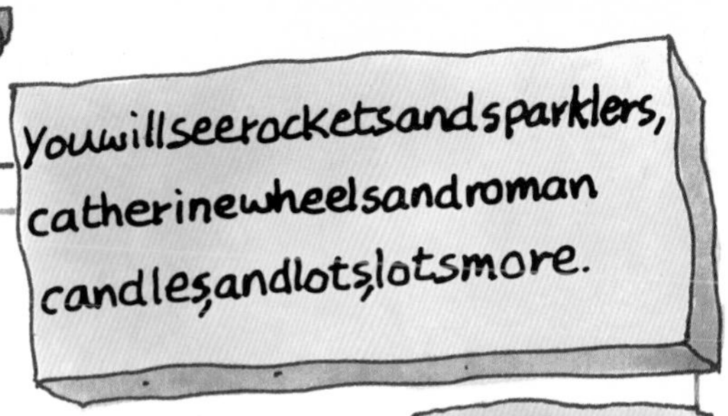

Full stops and capital letters

The Og family leave messages for each other on the kitchen wall. Can you write their messages for them, putting in full stops and capital letters in the correct places? Read the messages first and see where you need to leave a pause. Use full stops to mark these gaps, or pauses.

Leave a note for the milkman. Tell him to give us two jugs of beetle juice.

Mrs. Og

A full stop tells you where to leave a gap, or pause, when you are reading.

leave a note for the milkman tell him to give us two jugs of beetle juice
when you go shopping get my trousers from the cleaners I need them for the party
ring the theatre to book five tickets for the pantomime it is on next week

A word that comes straight after a full stop has to have a capital letter.
The first word of the note needs a capital letter as well.
please video the cookery programme tonight we can watch it tomorrow
the school concert starts at two o'clock don't be late
i need some more wool for Grandpa's new vest ten balls will do

Question marks

It is quiz night in the Hadrosaur's Head. Each team is warming up by shouting out questions and answers. Write in question marks after the questions and full stops after the answers.

You could show which answer matches each question by using a different coloured crayon for each question and answer pair.

They were painted by Leonardo da Ogtown
It's five stone-throws long
What do the letters O.B.B.C. stand for
She stayed at the Stalactite Hotel
Who teaches form five at Ogtown school
Whose pottery won first prize at last year's Ogtown Craft Show
You can buy them at the Caterpillar Café
The editor of the Ogtown News is Mog Og
In which street would you find Ogtown Fire Station

Commas in lists

The Ogs are going on holiday tomorrow. They are all busy packing and thinking of things to take and things to do before they go. Can you put the lists of things they are thinking about into sentences that remind them what they have to do?

There is no comma before the first word in the list, or after the last.

When there is a list of words in a sentence, each word in the list is separated from the next by a comma.

I must remember to check
petrol
water
oil
tyres

I must remember to check the petrol, water, oil and tyres.

The last word in the list is usually joined to the list by "and" instead of a comma.

Don't forget to put a full stop at the end of the sentence.

A comma tells you when to leave a short pause when you are reading. It marks a much shorter pause than a full stop.

I must go to the bank
supermarket
chemist
hairdresser

I must go to the

I need glue scissors pencils crayons for my scrapbook
I hope there's room for my spade bucket snorkel flippers surfboard
I'll need my paints brushes easel palette
I can't do without rich tea biscuits grapefruit marmalade peppermint teabags

I need

for my scrapbook

I hope there's room for my

I'll need my

I can't do without

Spaces and addresses

The Og family are on holiday in the Iguanodon Islands. They want to send postcards to their friends in Ogtown to tell them what they have been up to. They are thinking about what they want to write, but they are feeling lazy and sometimes they have run words together. Can you write their postcards for them, leaving a clear space between each word?

Isawa killershark
atthecoralreef
yesterday.

Dear Mig,
I saw a
killer shark
at the coral
reef yesterday.
Love Mog
Mig Ig
102 Reptile Road
Ogtown
OGT 1AA
Ogland

Lastnight
anenormousblackspider
crawledonto mybed.

Dear Miss Spell,
Love from
Zog

If you can't fit a whole word at the end of a line, don't split it in half. Put it all on the next line.

If you like you can put a comma at the end of each line of the address, except the last. Put a full stop at the end of the last line.

I had a ride on an enormous dinosaur. Will write again soon.

Can you fill in the addresses on the postcards. Write the name of the person it is going to on the first line, the number of the house and the road it is in on the second line, the town on the third line, the postcode on the fourth line, and the country on the last line.

Miss Spell's address is:

Ogtown School
Ogtown
OGT 2BB
Ogland

Dear Mrs. Ig,

Yours ever,
Mrs. Og

Dear Mr. Ig,

Best wishes,
Mr. Og

This morning I had a delicious breakfast of mango sausages.

Exclamation marks

Everyone in Ogtown has turned out to watch the match between the Ogtown Bashers and the Ugtown Mugs. Can you put exclamation marks in the speech bubbles, where they are needed? Be careful! Sometimes you might need to write a question mark instead.

An exclamation mark is used at the end of a sentence to mark surprise or excitement.
It can also show fear, anger, pain or danger.
When someone is giving an order, or shouting, an exclamation mark is used.
Oh no
Pass
Watch out
Stop him
Ouch
Are you alright
Tackle him
Go for it Bashers
Can we go now
Get off
What's the score
Foul
Where am I

Apostrophe s

Use an apostrophe followed by an s after the owner's name.
An apostrophe looks like a comma, but you put it near the top of a letter, instead of on the line.
Look at page 4 to help you decide who is the owner of each object.

The Ogs are moving to a new cave. They have packed up all their possessions and the removal men are just about to take them away. Can you write on the labels to show who each thing belongs to? Mog has already written on one of hers.

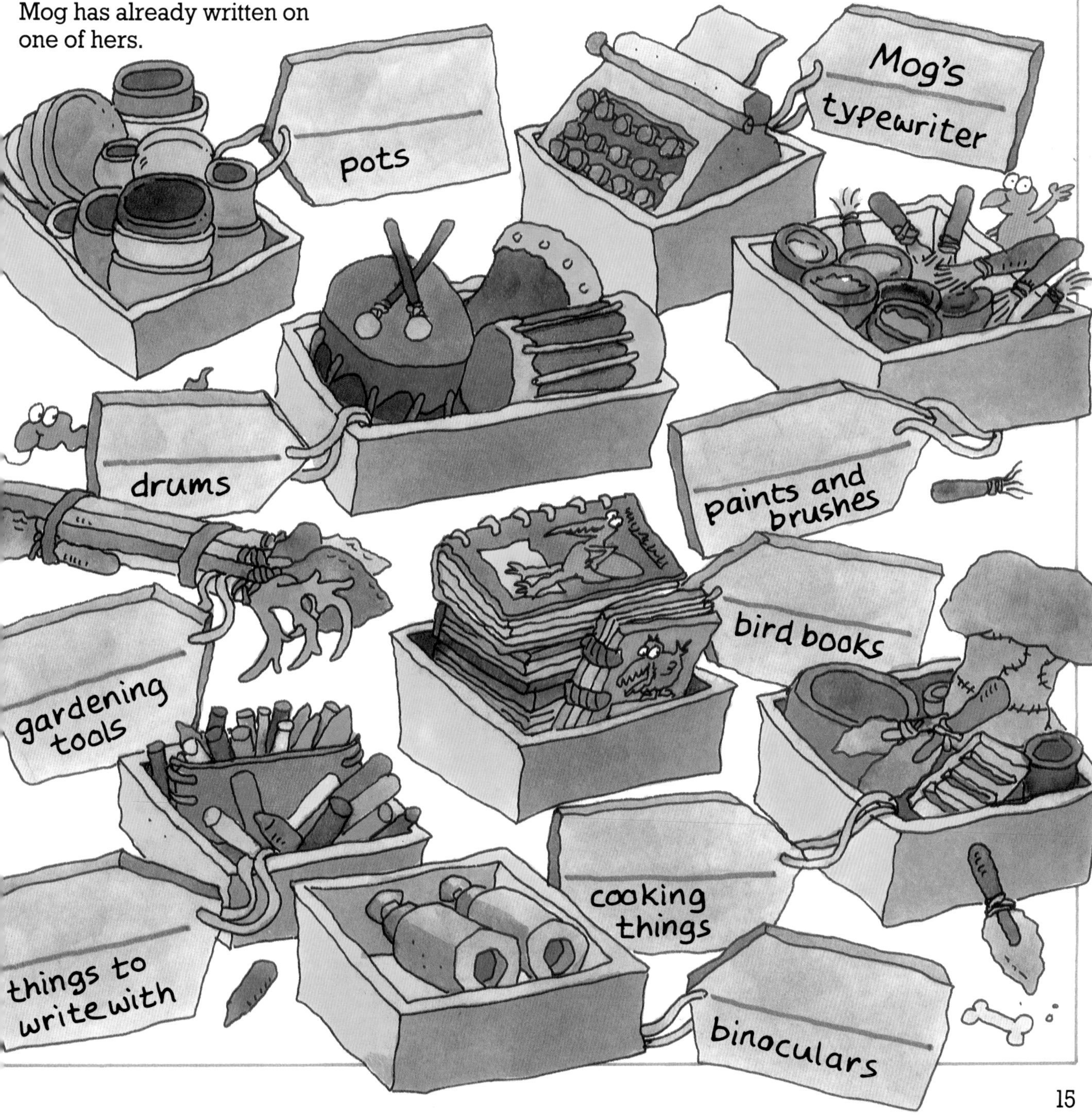
pots
Mog's typewriter
drums
paints and brushes
bird books
gardening tools
cooking things
things to write with
binoculars

Inverted commas

There has been an accident on Reptile Road. Sergeant Stig, of the Ogtown Police force, is taking notes about the accident to help him write a report.

Can you help Sergeant Stig by writing down what each witness said, between the inverted commas, in his notebook?

To show the exact words that someone has spoken, you put inverted commas round them. Inverted commas look like this “ ”.

Don't forget to start with a capital letter.

“ ,” said Grandma Og.

“ ,” shouted the fat man with red hair.

“ ,” cried the girl with long black hair.

“ ,” said the woman with the long necklace.

“ ,” said the driver in the red shirt.

Can you put in inverted commas to make these sentences easier to read?

There should be a speed limit, said the lady with the shopping basket.

Call the ambulance! shouted the old man with white hair.

My arm is hurting, said the boy on the skate board.

This lamp post is bent, said the girl with the skipping rope.

Where's my hat? said the lady with the spectacles.

Apostrophes to shorten words

Grandma Og refuses to use apostrophes to shorten words. Grandpa, on the other hand, shortens everything he possibly can. As a result they are constantly correcting each other. Can you fill in the missing speech bubbles in each pair? The first one has been done for you.

An apostrophe often means that two words have been joined together and that one or more letters have been left out. The apostrophe always goes in the place where one or more letters have been left out.

You're snoring.
We are having stew.
I'll be back soon.
I can't find it.
We're going too fast.
Who is at the door?

More on capitals

Here are some pages from Mog's diary. Her punctuation is good, but she still forgets to use capital letters. Put a line through each letter that should be a capital and write a capital letter above it.

The word "I" is always a capital letter.

People's names and place names always start with capital letters.

The days of the week and months of the year need capital letters as well.

monday november 11th

i was late for school today. sergeant stig stopped me in blaze street to ask if i had seen the accident in reptile road last tuesday.

tuesday november 12th

we went on a school outing to icthyosaur lake. the coach broke down in moss valley. lucy ug was sick and mr. slug fell in the lake.

wednesday november 13th

we are doing a project about spiders. miss spell let us go to bonehead library to do some research. i have written ten pages.

Don't forget to use a capital letter to start each new sentence.

The names of newspapers, magazines, books, plays and television programmes always start with a capital letter.

Christmas and Easter start with capital letters.

thursday november 14th

at school we had a rehearsal for our christmas play, the mammoth hunt. tig ig has got the best part. he is going to be the mammoth. i am one of the hunters.

friday november 15th

miss spell has made me stay in in break today because she caught me reading fitness freak under my desk. she made me learn a poem called the naughty girl. i hate her.

iss spell

saturday november 16th

i watched blue fred today. it's my favourite television programme. it's on every saturday morning. the presenters are called holly, bramble and thorn.

sunday november 17th

i wrote a book review for the ogtown news today. the book is called the secret of the painted caves. zog has promised to write about the ogtown basher's match.

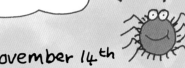

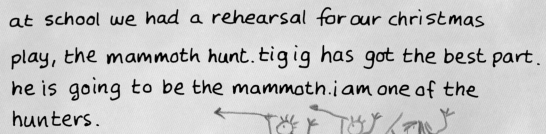

Commas in long sentences

Zog and his friends are playing a game. They are making up a story by taking it in turns to draw a picture and then write a sentence on Mog's typewriter to go with it. They have written quite long sentences, but they have forgotten to put in any commas. Can you find the right place for a comma in each sentence and write one in?

A comma shows where to make a slight pause when you are reading.

Say each sentence aloud to yourself. Where is the best place to divide it?

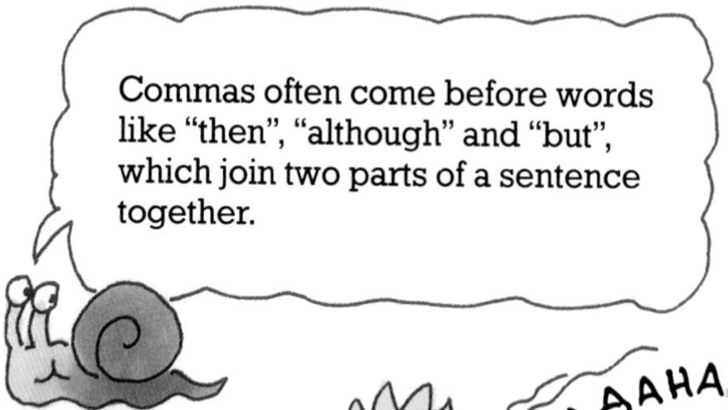
Commas often come before words like "then", "although" and "but", which join two parts of a sentence together.

A huge gorilla escaped from Ogtown zoo yesterday even though his keeper was sure he had locked the cage door.

While Mr. Og was peeling the potatoes he spotted the gorilla swinging on the washing line.

When Miss Spell saw the gorilla sitting at the back of her classroom she let out a piercing scream.

Sergeant Stig could hardly believe his eyes although he had been warned that a gorilla had escaped.

Zog Og gave the gorilla a ride on his skateboard but they ended up in the hedge.

The gorilla had tea at the Caterpillar Café then he returned to the zoo for a good night's sleep.

Commas with inverted commas

Mr. Slug is speaking to the whole school at the end of term assembly. Zog is writing a report of this occasion for Mog's newspaper, The Ogtown News. Can you write the words Mr Slug spoke inside the inverted commas in Zog's notebook? Separate the words in the inverted commas from the words in the rest of the sentence with a comma.

Words in inverted commas need separating from the rest of the sentence by a comma.
When the words in inverted commas come first in the sentence, the comma goes inside the inverted commas.
When the words spoken don't come first in the sentence, the comma goes before the inverted commas.
The first word spoken has a capital letter.
You have all worked hard this term.
Pog's Progress
Read Pog's Progress before next term.
We will now sing the school song.
Pog's Progress

End of Term Assembly

Everyone gathered in the school hall.

" ________________________________ ," said Mr. Slug.

Then he held up a book and said, " ________________________________

________________ ."

Everyone groaned, " ________________________________ ,"

he said as he stepped forwards and fell off the stage.

Mog's newspaper

Mog Og has started a newspaper. She has already completed one issue, with the help of her family and friends. Now they are working on the second issue.

IMPORTANT NOTE

Write two words instead of these words.

I'll ______

that's ______

they've ______

won't ______

didn't ______

you've ______

couldn't ______

who's ______

Mog has sent a note to everyone who is helping her, telling them not to use shortened words. Can you help them by writing the words they should use instead beside the shortened words on the list above?

Zog managed to get an interview with the glamorous actress, Dalores Dare, who was staying at the Stalactite Hotel. Mig Ig helped him by writing down what they said. Can you put in commas and inverted commas in Mig's notebook where necessary?

How are you enjoying your visit to Ogtown? said Zog.

I think Ogtown is a charming little place. The people are so friendly said Dalores.

Do you think The Fossil Saga was the right choice of play for Ogtown? said Zog.

The audience adored it. They laughed in all the funny bits and cried in all the sad bits said Dalores.

Did you find it difficult playing the part of Griselda? said Zog.

No. As soon as I read the play I understood her completely said Dalores.

Mrs. Og has started a cave painting business. She held an exhibition of her paintings to help to launch her business and Mog wrote a report on it for the Ogtown News. Can you put in five full stops to break the report into six sentences? After each full stop cross out the small letter and replace it with a capital.

Mrs. Og held an
exhibition of her
paintings last week
this was to celebrate
the opening of her new
business, Ogtown Interiors
her brilliant colours
and lively designs
caused much excitement
her prices are very
reasonable she promises
a quick service with no
mess for more information
ring 001122.

Grandpa has contributed some jokes for the newspaper. Can you fill in the missing question marks? Can you also suggest places where there might be full stops?

Knock, knock
Who's there
Felix
Felix who
Felixtremely cold

Knock, knock
Who's there
Alex
Alex who
Alex plain later
when you let me in

Grandpa

Letters to Mog

In the first issue Mog invited her readers to write and tell the newspaper about their problems. She has printed the letters she received together with her replies. Each letter is missing four punctuation marks. Can you put them in?

Ask Mog....

Dear Mog,

My grandpa plays very loud music when I m doing my homework I can't concentrate What do you suggest

Love from

Zog

Dear Zog

Try using ear plugs You can make them from beeswax I m sure this will help.

Love from

Mog

Dear Mog,

On Tuesdays I have to take my swimming things my history books my violin and my sandwiches to school. I can t carry them all. Can you help

Love from

Tig Ig

Dear Tig

Ask Mig to carry your violin If she won t, you ll have to buy a backpack.

Love from

Mog

Dear Mog

I am meant to write down the things people tell me, but I write too slowly to keep up I have to leave blank spaces How can I learn to write more quickly

Best wishes from

Sergeant Stig

Dear Sergeant Stig,

Miss Spell has a writing class for slow writers Its after school on Mondays Shall I ask her if you can join in

With best wishes from

Mog

Dear Mog,

I cook lovely meals When they are ready I call my family It has all gone cold by the time they sit down I get very upset

With regards from

Mr. Ig

Dear Mr. Ig

No wonder you get upset Try blowing a whistle or ringing a bell That ll make them hurry up!

With regards from

Mog

Answers

Page 3

8 Full stops

6 Question marks

5 Commas

8 Exclamation marks

2 Pairs of Inverted commas

Page 5

Pages 6 and 7

Pages 8 and 9

Pages 10 and 11

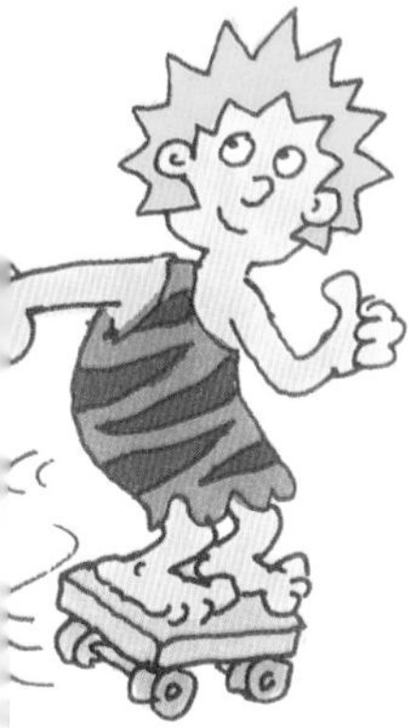

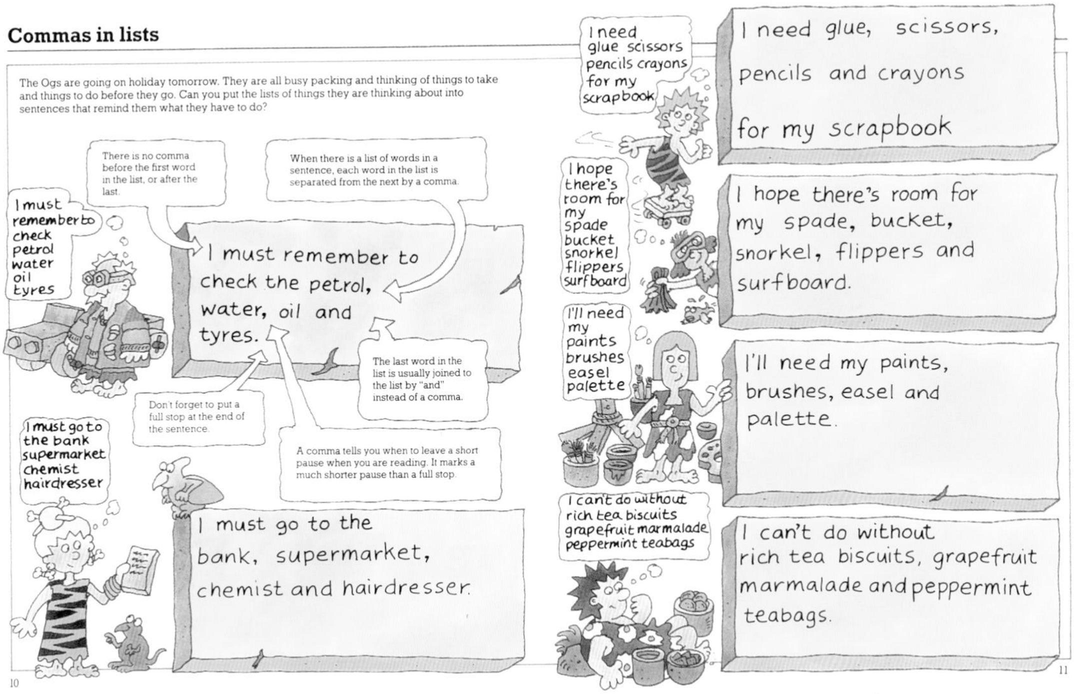

Pages 12 and 13

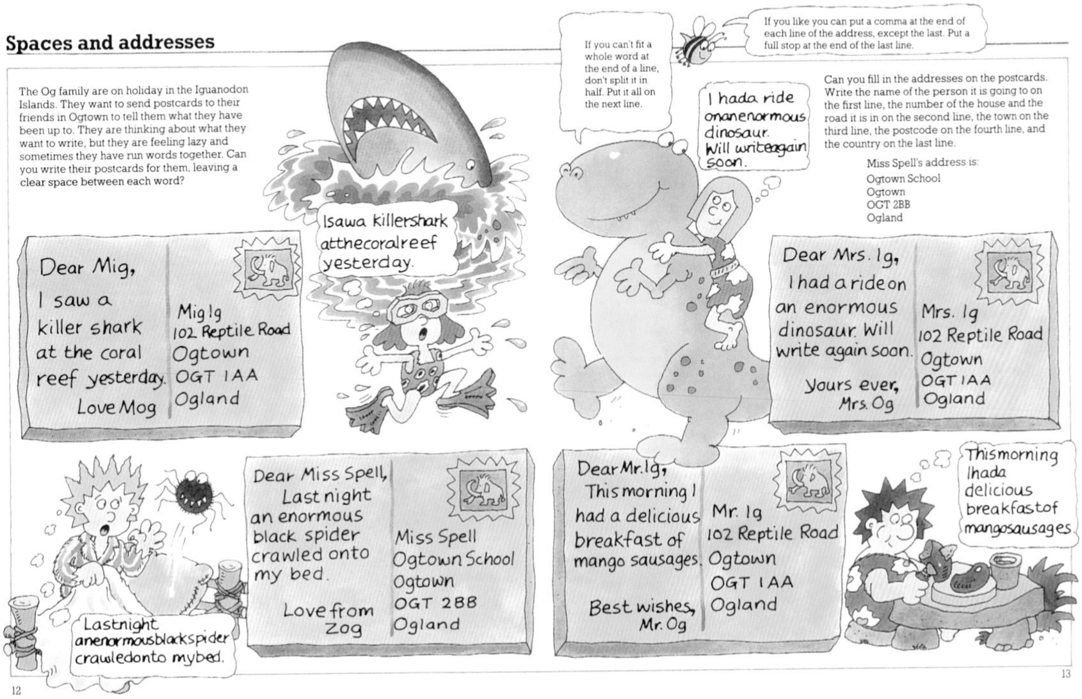

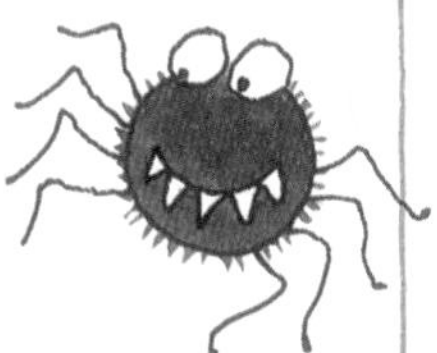

Page 14

Exclamation marks
Everyone in Ogtown has turned out to watch the match between the Ogtown Bashers and the Ugtown Mugs. Can you put exclamation marks in the speech bubbles, where they are needed? Be careful! Sometimes you might need to write a question mark instead.
An exclamation mark is used at the end of a sentence to mark surprise or excitement.
It can also show fear, anger, pain or danger.
When someone is giving an order, or shouting, an exclamation mark is used.
Oh no!
Pass!
Watch out!
Stop him!
Ouch!
Tackle him!
Are you alright?
Go for it Bashers!
Can we go now?
Get off!
What's the score?
Foul!
Where am I?
14

Pages 16 and 17

Inverted commas
There has been an accident on Reptile Road. Sergeant Stig, of the Ogtown Police force, is taking notes about the accident to help him write a report.
Can you help Sergeant Stig by writing down what each witness said, between the inverted commas, in his notebook?
To show the exact words that someone has spoken, you put inverted commas round them. Inverted commas look like this " ".
Don't forget to start with a capital letter.
Where's my hat?
The lamp post is bent.
Call the ambulance!
The grey car should have stopped.
The brown car was going too fast.
My arm is hurting.
There should be a speed limit.
It was his fault.
My brakes aren't working.
He nearly ran me over.
"The brown car was going too fast," said Grandma Og.
"The grey car should have stopped," shouted the fat man with red hair.
"He nearly ran me over," cried the girl with long black hair.
"It was his fault," said the woman with the long necklace.
"My brakes aren't working," said the driver in the red shirt.
Can you put in inverted commas to make these sentences easier to read?
"There should be a speed limit," said the lady with the shopping basket.
"Call the ambulance!" shouted the old man with white hair.
"My arm is hurting," said the boy on the skate board.
"This lamp post is bent," said the girl with the skipping rope.
"Where's my hat?" said the lady with the spectacles.
16
17

Page 15

Apostrophe s
The Ogs are moving to a new cave. They have packed up all their possessions and the removal men are just about to take them away. Can you write on the labels to show who each thing belongs to? Mog has already written on one of hers.
Use an apostrophe followed by an s after the owner's name.
An apostrophe looks like a comma, but you put it near the top of a letter, instead of on the line.
Look at page 4 to help you decide who is the owner of each object.
Grandma's pots
Mog's typewriter
Zog's drums
Mrs. Og's paints and brushes
Grandpa's bird books
Mr. Og's gardening tools
Mr. Og's cooking things
Mog's things to write with
Grandpa's binoculars

Grandma's
pots

Pages 18 and 19

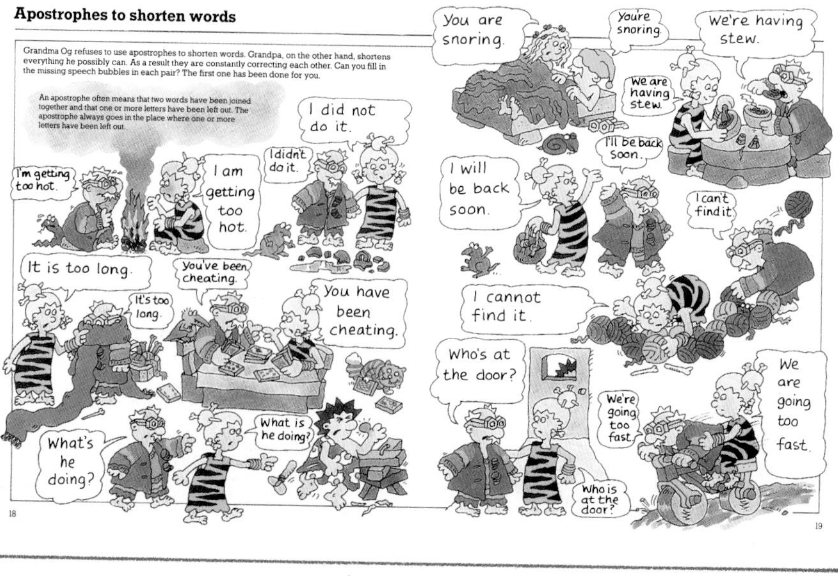
Apostrophes to shorten words
Grandma Og refuses to use apostrophes to shorten words. Grandpa, on the other hand, shortens everything he possibly can. As a result they are constantly correcting each other. Can you fill in the missing speech bubbles in each pair? The first one has been done for you.
An apostrophe often means that two words have been joined together and that one or more letters have been left out. The apostrophe always goes in the place where one or more letters have been left out.
I'm getting too hot.
I am getting too hot.
I didn't do it.
I did not do it.
It is too long.
It's too long.
You've been cheating.
You have been cheating.
What's he doing?
What is he doing?
You are snoring.
You're snoring.
We're having stew.
We are having stew.
I will be back soon.
I'll be back soon.
I can't find it.
I cannot find it.
Who's at the door?
Who is at the door?
We're going too fast.
We are going too fast.
18
19

Pages 20 and 21

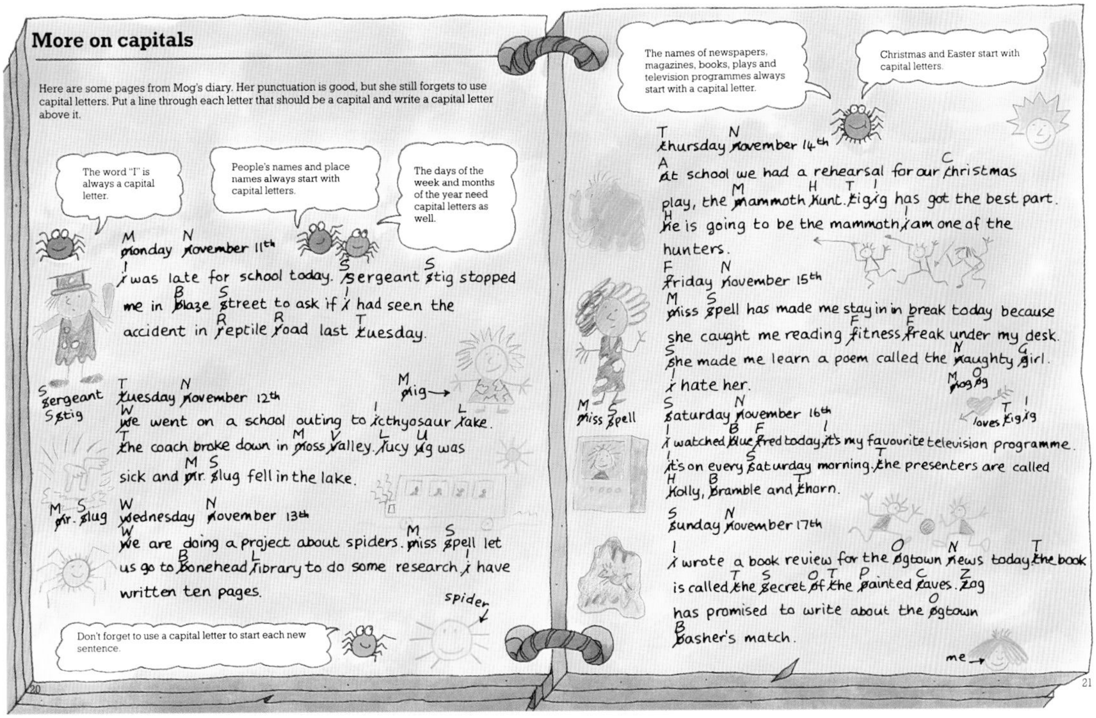

More on capitals

Here are some pages from Mog's diary. Her punctuation is good, but she still forgets to use capital letters. Put a line through each letter that should be a capital and write a capital letter above it.

The word "I" is always a capital letter.
People's names and place names always start with capital letters.
The days of the week and months of the year need capital letters as well.
Monday November 11th
I was late for school today. Sergeant Stig stopped me in Blaze Street to ask if I had seen the accident in Reptile Road last Tuesday.
Sergeant Stig
Mig
Tuesday November 12th
We went on a school outing to Icthyosaur Lake. The coach broke down in Moss Valley. Lucy Ug was sick and Mr. Slug fell in the lake.
Mr. Slug
Wednesday November 13th
We are doing a project about spiders. Miss Spell let us go to Bonehead Library to do some research. I have written ten pages.
spider
Don't forget to use a capital letter to start each new sentence.
20
The names of newspapers, magazines, books, plays and television programmes always start with a capital letter.
Christmas and Easter start with capital letters.
Thursday November 14th
At school we had a rehearsal for our Christmas play, the Mammoth Hunt. Tig has got the best part. He is going to be the mammoth. I am one of the hunters.
Friday November 15th
Miss Spell has made me stay in in break today because she caught me reading Fitness Freak under my desk. She made me learn a poem called the Naughty Girl. I hate her.
Mog Og
Miss Spell
loves Tig
Saturday November 16th
I watched Blue Fred today. It's my favourite television programme. It's on every Saturday morning. The presenters are called Holly, Bramble and Thorn.
Sunday November 17th
I wrote a book review for the Ogtown News today. The book is called The Secret Of The Painted Caves. Zog has promised to write about the Ogtown Basher's match.
me
21

miss spell

Pages 22 and 23

Commas in long sentences

Zog and his friends are playing a game. They are making up a story by taking it in turns to draw a picture and then write a sentence on Mog's typewriter to go with it. They have written quite long sentences, but they have forgotten to put in any commas. Can you find the right place for a comma in each sentence and write one in?

A comma shows where to make a slight pause when you are reading.
Say each sentence aloud to yourself. Where is the best place to divide it?
Commas often come before words like "then", "although" and "but", which join two parts of a sentence together.
AAAAAHA!

A huge gorilla escaped from Ogtown zoo yesterday, even though his keeper was sure he had locked the cage door.

While Mr. Og was peeling the potatoes, he spotted the gorilla swinging on the washing line.

When Miss Spell saw the gorilla sitting at the back of her classroom, she let out a piercing scream.

Sergeant Stig could hardly believe his eyes, although he had been warned that a gorilla had escaped.

Zog Og gave the gorilla a ride on his skateboard, but they ended up in the hedge.

The gorilla had tea at the Caterpillar Café, then he returned to the zoo for a good night's sleep.

22

Commas with inverted commas

Mr. Slug is speaking to the whole school at the end of term assembly. Zog is writing a report of this occasion for Mog's newspaper, The Ogtown News. Can you write the words Mr Slug spoke inside the inverted commas in Zog's notebook? Separate the words in the inverted commas from the words in the rest of the sentence with a comma.

Words in inverted commas need separating from the rest of the sentence by a comma.
When the words in inverted commas come first in the sentence, the comma goes inside the inverted commas.
When the words spoken don't come first in the sentence, the comma goes before the inverted commas.
The first word spoken has a capital letter.
You have all worked hard this term.
Read Pog's Progress before next term.
We will now sing the school song.
Pog's Progress

End of Term Assembly

Everyone gathered in the school hall.

"You have all worked hard this term," said Mr. Slug. Then he held up a book and said, "Read Pog's Progress before next term." Everyone groaned, "We will now sing the school song," he said as he stepped forwards and fell off the stage.

23

Pages 24 and 25

Mog's newspaper

Mog Og has started a newspaper. She has already completed one issue, with the help of her family and friends. Now they are working on the second issue.

IMPORTANT NOTE
Write two words instead of these words.

I'll	I will
that's	that is
they've	they have
won't	will not
didn't	did not
you've	you have
couldn't	could not
who's	who is

Mog has sent a note to everyone who is helping her, telling them not to use shortened words. Can you help them by writing the words they should use instead beside the shortened words on the list above?

Zog managed to get an interview with the glamorous actress, Dalores Dare, who was staying at the Stalactite Hotel. Mig Ig helped him by writing down what they said. Can you put in commas and inverted commas in Mig's notebook where necessary?

"How are you enjoying your visit to Ogtown?" said Zog.
"I think Ogtown is a charming little place. The people are so friendly," said Dalores.
"Do you think The Fossil Saga was the right choice of play for Ogtown?" said Zog.
"The audience adored it. They laughed in all the funny bits and cried in all the sad bits," said Dalores.
"Did you find it difficult playing the part of Griselda?" said Zog.
"No. As soon as I read the play I understood her completely," said Dalores.

24

Mrs. Og has started a cave painting business. She held an exhibition of her paintings to help to launch her business and Mog wrote a report on it for the Ogtown News. Can you put in five full stops to break the report into six sentences? After each full stop cross out the small letter and replace it with a capital.

Mrs. Og held an exhibition of her paintings last week. This was to celebrate the opening of her new business, Ogtown Interiors. Her brilliant colours and lively designs caused much excitement. Her prices are very reasonable. She promises a quick service with no mess. For more information ring 001122.

Grandpa has contributed some jokes for the newspaper. Can you fill in the missing question marks? Can you also suggest places where there might be full stops?

Knock, knock.	Knock, knock.
Who's there?	Who's there?
Felix.	Alex.
Felix who?	Alex who?
Felixtremely cold.	Alex plain later when you let me in.
	Grandpa

Pages 26 and 27

Letters to Mog

In the first issue Mog invited her readers to write and tell the newspaper about their problems. She has printed the letters she received together with her replies. Each letter is missing four punctuation marks. Can you put them in?

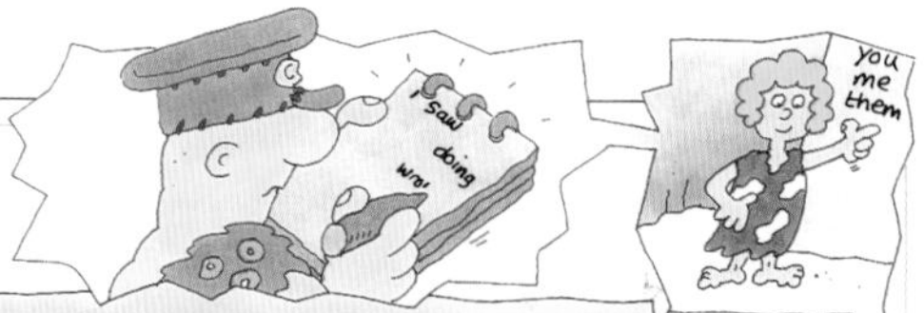

Ask Mog....

Dear Mog,

My grandpa plays very loud music when I'm doing my homework. I can't concentrate. What do you suggest?

Love from

Zog

Dear Zog,

Try using ear plugs. You can make them from beeswax. I'm sure this will help.

Love from

Mog

Dear Mog,

On Tuesdays I have to take my swimming things, my history books, my violin and my sandwiches to school. I can't carry them all. Can you help?

Love from

Tig Ig

Dear Tig,

Ask Mig to carry your violin. If she won't, you'll have to buy a backpack.

Love from

Mog

Dear Mog,

I am meant to write down the things people tell me, but I write too slowly to keep up. I have to leave blank spaces. How can I learn to write more quickly?

Best wishes from

Sergeant Stig

Dear Sergeant Stig,

Miss Spell has a writing class for slow writers. It's after school on Mondays. Shall I ask her if you can join in?

With best wishes from

Mog

Dear Mog,

I cook lovely meals. When they are ready I call my family. It has all gone cold by the time they sit down. I get very upset.

With regards from

Mr. Ig

Dear Mr. Ig,

No wonder you get upset. Try blowing a whistle or ringing a bell. That'll make them hurry up!

With regards from

Mog

26

27